P9-DNR-823

Grandma Drove the Garbage Truck

Written by
Katie Clark

Illustrated by
Amy Huntington

Down East Books
Camden, Maine

Text copyright © 2005 by Katie Clark
Illustrations copyright © 2005
by Amy Huntington

Printed in China

2   4   5   3   1

Down East Books
Camden, Maine
a division of Down East Enterprise
Book orders: 800-685-7962
www.downeastbooks.com

Library of Congress Cataloging-
in-Publication Data

Clark, Katie, 1962-
Grandma drove the garbage truck / story by Katie
Clark ; illustrated by Amy Huntington.
    p. cm.
    Summary: Because her three sons are sick,
Grandma drives the garbage truck on the Fourth of
July, ending up with an award in the big parade.
    ISBN 0-89272-698-9 (trade hardcover : alk. paper)
    [1. Refuse collection vehicles--Fiction. 2. Grand-
mothers--Fiction. 3. Parades--Fiction. 4. Fourth of
July--Fiction.] I. Huntington, Amy, ill. II. Title.
    PZ7.C54823Gra 2006
    [E]--dc22

2005027440

To Rob, Daniel, and Ellie;
and with special thanks to
Bea Hudon, my inspiration

— K.C.

For Ward and Mona

— A.H.

Rrring!

Grandma slapped the
alarm clock beside her bed.

Rrring!!

Grandma opened one eye.
She slapped the alarm clock again.

Rrring!!!

It wasn't the alarm clock. It was the telephone!

"Hello," yawned Grandma.

"Ah-choo!" sneezed a voice.

"Ma, I'm sick, sick as a dog. My stomach's churning,
my eyes are burning, and my head's turning."

It was Buster, Grandma's first son.

"Ma, there's no way I can drive the . . . Ah-choo! . . . truck this morning."

Grandma squinted at the calendar tacked beside her bed.

"Parade Day, of all days!" she scolded. "Well, never mind.
We'll do fine without you. Get some rest, Buster.
And Buster, for goodness sake, use your handkerchief!"
Grandma hung up the phone.

Grandma had been in the garbage business for as far back as anyone could remember. She ran the office: answering the phone, opening the mail, and counting the money. Her three sons drove the trucks.

For Grandma, and everyone else, there was no bigger holiday than the 4th of July. Folks prepared for months: building fancy floats, practicing marching songs, buying new outfits, hanging up flags. The town had to look spic and span for the Big Parade!

Grandma stretched and hopped out of bed.

Rrring!

Rrring!!

Rrring!!!

Grandma held her toothbrush in one hand and picked up the phone with the other.

"Hello?" she burbled.

"Coff–off!" coughed a voice. "Ma, I'm sick, sick as a dog. My eyes are burning, my head's turning, and my stomach's churning."

It was Burt, Grandma's second son.

"Ma, there's no way I can run the . . . Coff—off! . . . compactor this morning."

Grandma glanced at the clock on the shelf.

"The parade starts at 10 o'clock," fretted Grandma. "Well, never mind. We can manage without you. Get some rest, Burt. And Burt, for goodness sake, cover your mouth when you cough!" Grandma hung up the phone.

Brring!

Grandma held her coffee mug in one hand and answered the phone with the other.

"Hello!" spluttered Grandma.

Brring!!

"Hello?!"

Brring!!!

It wasn't the telephone. It was the doorbell. There at the door stood Bill, Grandma's third and last son, with little Billy at his side. Bill didn't have to say a word. Grandma could tell his head was turning, his stomach was churning, and his eyes were burning. Bill was sick, sick as a dog. There was no way he could drive a truck much less run the compactor.

"Shameful, just shameful, making folks parade past garbage on the 4th of July!" muttered Grandma. "Well, never mind. Come in, Bill. And Bill, for goodness sake, sit yourself down in my comfy chair."

Grandma eyed Bill. Then she eyed her littlest grandson. Thank goodness, he looked healthy as a horse.

Grandma grabbed a pair of Buster's old coveralls. She tossed her grandson a pair of greasy gloves. "It looks like we've got a job to do, Billy," she said. "A BIG JOB!"

Grandma clapped on Bert's best baseball cap and shoved her feet, slippers and all, into Bill's work boots. Billy ran to fetch three cushions from the couch—one for him and two for Grandma.

Grandma gave Billy a boost. Then Billy gave Grandma a hand.

Grandma peered through the steering wheel.

"I sure hope I can drive this big, old clunker!" Grandma hollered as she revved the engine and released the brake. The garbage truck zoomed down the driveway.

"The mailbox! The mailbox!" screamed Billy.

But Grandma didn't hear.
She was too busy looking to the left.

The garbage truck skidded around the bend.

"My roses! My roses!" shouted Roy Hardy.

But Grandma didn't hear. She was too busy hauling trash cans.

The garbage truck bumped down the lane.

"My clothesline! My clothesline!" shrieked Edna Fillmore.

But Grandma didn't hear. She was too busy working the compactor.

The garbage truck raced across the avenue.

"My flag! My flag!" squealed little Maggie Wells.

But Grandma didn't hear. She was too busy backing up.

The garbage truck swerved onto Main Street.

"The parade! The parade!" yelled Billy. "THE PARADE!"

Grandma stood on the brake. But . . . too late!

The garbage truck screeched to a stop right in front of the All-Star Marching Band!

Grandma adjusted her glasses and tipped her cap. Banners, flags, and hats waved back.

Grandma tapped the horn. Flutes, trumpets, and trombones tooted an encore.

Grandma thumped Billy on the back. "I guess I can drive this big, old clunker any day," she chuckled.

"Three cheers for Grandma!" shouted Billy.

Then he scrambled up the front fender of the garbage truck. He proudly nestled the blue ribbon for "Most Creative Float" in a wreath of Roy Hardy's best roses.

What a perfect day for a parade.